Get your daily dose of Dad Jokes on
Instagram, Twitter and Facebook.

## @DADJOKEBUTTON

Greetings reader,

My wife said, "Why don't you stop telling terrible Dad Jokes and write a book instead?" Thank you dear, for such a novel idea. Introducing, The Dad Joke Novel!

This book is similar to the book on Stockholm syndrome that I've been reading. It was pretty bad at first, but by the end I liked it.

Or that book about anti-gravity that's impossible to put down.

I must leave you with a word of caution about reading this book! It left me with an awful headache after it fell on my head. But I only have my shelf to blame.

Enough with the outrageously painful book puns! Thank you, kind reader, for supporting The Dad Joke Novel. I hope you enjoy this Dad's favorite 500 hilariously groan-worthy jokes.

Sincerely,
Dad

**I was going to jump rope for exercise this morning.**

But I ended up skipping it.

**My twin brother called me from prison.**

He said, "Do you know how we finish each other's sentences?"

**Today, my son asked, "Can I have a bookmark?" and I burst into tears.**

11 years old and he still doesn't know my name is Brian.

**I got an e-mail saying, "At Google Earth, we can read maps backwards!"**

I thought, "That's just spam!"

**My wife screamed, "You haven't listened to a single word I've said, have you?!"**

What a weird way to start a conversation.

**I have a fear of speed bumps.**

I'm slowly getting over it.

**I have a fear of elevators.**

But I've started taking steps to avoid it.

**I used to be addicted to the Hokey Pokey.**

But then I turned myself around.

**What do you call a man with no nose and no body?**

Nobody nose.

## What do you call a man with no arms and no legs lying in front of your door?

Matt.

## What do you call twins with no arms and no legs holding up the drapes?

Curt and Rod.

## What do you call a man with no arms and no legs wiggling in a pile of leaves?

Russell.

## What do you call a woman with one leg longer than the other?

Eileen.

## Son: How many apples grow on a tree?

Dad: All of them.

## Son: Did you get a haircut?

Dad: No, I got them all cut.

**My daughter said she was cold.**

**So, I told her to sit in the corner.**

Because it's 90 degrees.

**Have you heard about the restaurant on the moon?**

Great food, no atmosphere.

**Waitress: Careful, that plate is hot!**

Dad: It's okay, I'm not attracted to the plate.

**Waitress: Careful, that plate is hot!**

Dad: It's okay, so am I.

**What's the best day to cook?**

Fryday.

**What's orange and sounds like a parrot?**

A carrot.

**Want to hear a joke about paper?**

Never mind, it's terrible.

**I used to work in a shoe recycling shop.**

It was sole destroying.

**There's a new type of broom out.**

It's sweeping the nation.

## My friend David lost his ID.

Now I call him Dav.

## What days are the strongest?

Saturday and Sunday, the rest are week days.

## I was just looking at my ceiling.

Not sure if it's the best ceiling in the world, but it's definitely up there.

## Why did the partially blind man fall into the well?

Because he couldn't see that well.

## Anyone want to buy a broken barometer?

No pressure.

## Whoever stole my anti-depressants...

I hope you're happy now.

**Yesterday I slapped Dwayne Johnson's ass.**

I've officially hit rock bottom.

DAD JOKE #32

**Last time when I was someone's type...**

I was donating blood.

DAD JOKE #33

**I've got this awful disease where I can't stop telling airport jokes.**

The doctor says it's terminal.

**Did you know that 97% of the world is stupid?**

Luckily, I'm in the other 5%.

**Why don't skeletons ever go trick or treating?**

Because they have no body to go with.

**What's the leading cause of dry skin?**

Towels.

## Rest in peace boiled water.

You will be mist.

## I don't trust stairs.

They're always up to something.

## What do you call a fat psychic?
A four-chin teller.

DAD JOKE #40

**I was in my garden and saw 10 ants running frantically. So, I made them a little house out of cardboard.**

I guess that makes me their landlord and them… my tenants.

DAD JOKE #41

**I used to hate facial hair.**

But then it grew on me.

DAD JOKE #42

**Found out I was color blind the other day.**

That one came right out the purple…

**A man tried to sell me a coffin today.**

I told him that's the last thing I need.

**When my wife told me to stop impersonating a flamingo.**

I had to put my foot down.

**Singing in the shower is all fun and games until you get shampoo in your mouth.**

Then it's a soap opera.

## The rotation of earth...

really makes my day.

## You can't run through a camp site.

You can only ran, because it's past tents.

## You heard the rumor going around about butter?

Never mind, I shouldn't spread it.

**Parallel lines have so much in common.**

It's a shame they'll never meet.

DAD JOKE #50

**I asked my wife if I was the only one she'd been with.**

She said yes, all the others had been nines and tens.

DAD JOKE #51

**I recently started a band called 999 Megabytes.**

We're good but we haven't got a gig yet...

**Why is "Dark" spelled with a K, and not a C?**

Because you can't C in the dark.

**Saw a man standing on one leg at an ATM.**

**I asked him what he was doing.**

He said, "Just checking my balance."

**What's blue and doesn't weigh very much?**

Light blue.

**My wife complains I don't buy her flowers.**

To be honest, I didn't know she sold flowers.

DAD JOKE #56

**Chinese takeaway - $20.**

**Cost of delivery - $2**

**Getting home to find out they've forgotten part of your order?**

Riceless.

**I named my horse mayo...**

Mayo neighs.

**Which is heavier:**

**A liter of water or a liter of butane?**

**The water.**

No matter how much you have, butane will always be a lighter fluid.

## Police have arrested the world tongue-twister champion.

They said he'll be given a tough sentence.

## Welcome to the plastic surgery addicts' group.

I see a lot of new faces here today.

**Three years ago, my doctor told me I was going deaf.**

I haven't heard from him since.

**I'm reading a horror story in Braille.**

Something bad is going to happen.
I can feel it.

**Did you hear about the chameleon who couldn't change color?**

He had a reptile dysfunction.

**I don't often tell dad jokes.**

But when I do, he usually laughs.

**The creator of the knock, knock joke should get...**

a No Bell prize.

**Where are all these great dad jokes stored?**

The dadabase.

**You've really gotta hand it to short people...**

Because they usually can't reach it anyway.

**My boss is going to fire the employee with the worst posture.**

I have a hunch, it might be me.

**Why can't you use "Beef Stew" as a password?**

Because it's not stroganoff.

## If a child refuses to sleep during nap time...

Does that mean they're guilty of resisting a rest?

## I had an interview at a scissor factory today.

Unfortunately, I didn't make the cut.

## As I reflect back on my past, I remember the time when I forgot to pay my electric bill.

Those were some dark days.

**I heard on the news that some guy was stealing wheels off police cars.**

The police are working tirelessly to catch him

**Don't trust atoms.**

They make up everything.

**A blind person was eating sea food.**

It didn't help.

**I took up origami for a while.**

But I gave it up because it was too much paperwork.

**It's a 5-minute walk from my home to the pub. It's a 35-minute walk from the pub to my home.**

The difference is staggering.

**What's Forest Gump's Facebook password?**

1forest1

## Did you hear about the kidnapping at school?

It's ok, he woke up.

## I try to tell everyone about the benefits of eating dried grapes.

It's all about raisin' awareness.

## My doctor told me that I needed I kidney.

But I had to ask her if I could get an adult-knee instead.

**I was wondering why there was music coming from printer.**

Then I realized the paper was jammin'.

**What did Pink Panther say when he stepped on an ant?**

Dead ant.
Dead ant. Dead ant, dead ant, dead ant.

**A skeleton walked into a bar.**

He said I need a beer and a mop.

**I told my daughter to be careful standing next to those trees.**

They looked shady.

**Want to hear a chimney joke?**

Got stacks of them! First one's on the house.

**The other day, my wife asked me to pass her lipstick, but I accidentally passed her a glue stick.**

She still isn't talking to me.

**What do Zombie Cows say?**

Graaaiiins!

**I'm looking to sell my Delorean. It's in Great condition, low mileage.**

Only driven from time to time!

**I struggle with Roman Numerals until I get to 159.**

Then it just CLIX.

**The only thing flat earthers fear...**

is sphere itself.

**I just sat next to a baby on a 12-hour flight. I had no idea that someone could cry for 12 hours straight.**

Even the baby seemed impressed.

**The invention of the wheel was...**

revolutionary.

**The invention of the shovel was...**

groundbreaking.

DAD JOKE #95

**Bleeping a curse word is usually funnier than the word itself.**

Itself just isn't a very funny word.

DAD JOKE #96

**My wife agreed to finally watch Back to the future.**

I told her it's about time.

## What do you call it when a pirate has sore joints?

Arrrrrthritis.

## What does a pepper do when it gets angry?

It gets jalapeño your face.

## Why do cows have bells around their necks?

Because their horns don't work.

## What has two butts and kills people?

An assassin.

## What do you call a wolf that has things figured out?

Aware wolf.

## How do you wake up lady gaga?

Poker face.

**I was washing my car with my son.**

He said, "Can't you just use the sponge?"

**I interviewed for a job as a waiter. They asked me "So why do you think you'd make a good waiter".**

I said, "Well, I think I could bring a lot to the table".

**Sundays are always a little sad.**

But the day before is a sadder day.

## The person who invented autocorrect should burn in hello.

## My wife said nothing rhymes with orange.

I said no it doesn't.

## Rick Astley has a collection of every Pixar movie ever. And he'll let you borrow any of them. Except one.

He's never gonna give you *Up*.

**What do you call a fake noodle?**

An Impasta.

**What do you call a belt with a watch on it?**

A waist of time.

**I recently took an airline to court after my luggage didn't turn up.**

I lost my case.

## What do you call a pile of kittens?

A meowntain.

## We all know where the Big Apple is, but does anyone know where the...

Minneapolis?

## "Hey officer, how did the hackers escape?"

"No idea, they just ransomware".

**What do you call a beat-up Batman?**

A Bruised Wayne.

DAD JOKE #116

**How did the farmer find his daughter?**

Tractor.

DAD JOKE #117

**What cheese can never be yours?**

Nacho cheese.

## Why don't programmers carry guns?

They have troubleshooting.

## What is it called when one butt cheek is bigger than the other?

<u>Ass</u>ymmetrical.

## The internet connection in my farm was really sketchy, so I moved the modem to the barn.

Now I have stable Wi-Fi.

**My wife always yells at me for not knowing how to properly season my food, but I don't mind.**

I take it with a pinch of sugar.

**What do you get from a pampered cow?**

Spoiled milk.

**I saw a sign today that made me piss myself.**

It said, 'Toilets closed'.

## I really want to buy one of the grocery checkout dividers.

But the lady behind the counter keeps putting it back.

## Never fart in an Apple store.

They don't have any windows

## I can always tell when someone is lying just by looking at them.

I can tell when they're standing too.

**While visiting the museum, I saw my ex-girlfriend standing across the hall, but I was too self-conscious to say hello.**

There was just too much history between us.

**I think it's weird that we call childbirth delivery.**

It should have been called takeout instead.

**What's the fastest growing city on earth?**

The capital of Ireland. It's Dublin every day.

## My wife told me to take a spider out instead of killing it.

We went out and had beers. Cool guy, very driven, wants to be a web designer.

## For me, the urge to sing "The Lion Sleeps Tonight" is always just a whim away...

*a whim away, a whim away, a whim away, a whim away.*

## Of all the inventions of the last 100 years...

the dry erase board has to be the most remarkable.

## My wife kicked me out because of my terrible Arnold Schwarzenegger impressions. But don't worry...

I'll return.

## To be Frank, I'd have to change my name.

DAD JOKE #135

**People keep saying today is Pi day.**

But to me, March 14th will always be cake day.

DAD JOKE #136

**I got the words "jacuzzi" and "yakuza" confused.**

Now I'm in hot water with the Japanese mafia.

DAD JOKE #137

**Even though Spongebob is the main character...**

Patrick is the star.

## My eBay is so useless.

I tried to look up lighters and all they had was 13,749 matches.

## My wife traumatically ripped the blankets off me last night.

But I will recover.

## A storm blew away 25% of my roof last night

oof

**Two drunk guys were about to get into a fight.**

**One draws a line in the dirt and says, "If you cross this line, I'll hit you in the face."**

That was the punchline.

**Nothing's better than being 2, 3, 5, 7, 11, 13, 17, 19, 23, 29, 31, 37, 41, 43, 47, 53, 59, 61, 67, 71, 73, 79, 83, 89, or 97 years old.**

Those are the years you're in your prime.

**I was really embarrassed when my wife caught me playing with my son's train set by myself.**

**In a moment of panic, I threw a bedsheet over it.**

I think I managed to cover my tracks.

DAD JOKE #144

**Without geometry life is pointless.**

DAD JOKE #145

**On his deathbed, my grandfather said,
"Remember these two words.**

**They'll open a lot of doors for you in life."**

Push and Pull.

DAD JOKE #146

**People are usually shocked when they find
out I'm not a very good electrician.**

**My son was just born and another dad at the nursery congratulated me and said his daughter was born yesterday.**

**He said maybe they'll marry each other.**

Sure, like my son is going to marry someone twice his age.

**I was in a uber today and the driver said, "I love my job. I'm my own boss. Nobody tells me what to do."**

Then I said, "Turn left here."

DAD JOKE #149

**Did you hear about the guy whose whole left side was cut off?**

He's all right now.

DAD JOKE #150

**Why didn't the skeleton cross the road?**

Because he had no guts.

DAD JOKE #151

**What did one nut say as he chased another nut?**

I'm a cashew!

## Chances are if you've seen one shopping center...

you've seen a mall.

## I was warned not to steal kitchen utensils.

But it's a whisk I am willing to take.

## How come the stadium got hot after the game?

Because all of the fans left.

## Why was it called the dark ages?

Because of all the knights.

## A steak pun...

is a rare medium well done.

## Why did the tomato blush?

Because it saw the salad dressing.

DAD JOKE #158

## What creature is smarter than a talking parrot?

A spelling bee.

DAD JOKE #159

## I'll tell you what often gets overlooked...

Garden fences.

DAD JOKE #160

## My first time using an elevator was an uplifting experience.

The second time let me down.

## Slept like a log last night.

Woke up in the fireplace.

## Why does a Moon-rock taste better than an Earth-rock?

Because it's a little meteor.

## *Reverses car*

"Ahhhh, this takes me back."

**I broke my wrist yesterday and asked the doctor, "When this heals, will I be able to play the piano?"**

**The doc said, "Yes, you'll be fine in a few days."**

"Perfect, I've always wanted to be able to play an instrument."

**Wife: Call me a taxi!**

Dad: You're a taxi.

DAD JOKE #166

## The waitress asked me if I want a box for my leftover food.

I told her, "No, but I'll wrestle you for it"

DAD JOKE #167

## My daughter turned 18 today, so I bought her a locket and put her picture in it.

**As I gently placed it around her neck, choking back the tears, I said, "Well, sweetheart, I guess you really are...**

Independent."

**Did you know that all the people who live around here aren't allowed to be buried in that cemetery?**

Because they're not dead yet.

**You know you can tell whether an ant is a girl or a boy by dropping it in water?**

**If it sinks, it's a girl ant.**

If it floats, it's boy ant.

**A cannibal is someone who is fed up with people.**

# Why do chicken coops only have two doors?

Because if they had four, they would be chicken sedans.

# The waitress said to me, "Sorry about the wait".

Angrily, I said, "well I've been doing my best to lose it before swimsuit season".

## What's the difference between a hippo and a Zippo?

One is really heavy and the other is a little lighter.

## 6:30 is my favorite time of day.

Hands down.

## I was so bored I memorized six pages of a dictionary.

I learned next to nothing.

## What does Alexander the Great and Winnie the Pooh have in common?

They both have the same middle name

## I love my furniture.

My recliner and I go way back.

## You know Orion's Belt?

Big waist of space, huh?

**As I was ordering bacon and eggs, the waitress asked me, "How do you like your eggs?"**

I replied, "I haven't got them yet!"

**Why do graveyards have gates?**

Because people are dying to get in.

**A magician was walking down the street.**

Then, he turned into a grocery store.

**"Would you like the milk in the bag?"**

"No thanks, you can keep it in the carton."

**What happens to a frog's car when it breaks down?**

It gets toad.

**You know why you never see an elephant hiding in a tree?**

Because they're very good at it.

**What's green, furry, has 4 legs and will kill you if it falls out of a tree onto you?**

A pool table.

DAD JOKE #186

**What does a pirate say when he's 80?**

Aye matey.

DAD JOKE #187

**I thought my wife was joking when she said she'd leave me if I didn't stop signing "I'm A Believer"...**

Then I saw her face.

## Why is Peter Pan always flying?

Because he Neverlands.

## Did you know that protons have mass?

I didn't even know they were Catholic.

## I was fired from the keyboard factory yesterday.

I wasn't putting in enough shifts.

**My wife told me she was pregnant today.**

**She said we should go to the baby doctor.**

I said, "I think I'd be a lot more comfortable going to an adult doctor."

**Do I enjoy making courthouse puns?**

Guilty.

## Why did the kid throw the clock out the window?

He wanted to see time fly!

## Why couldn't the kid see the pirate movie?

Because it was rated arrr!

## Why did the man run around his bed?

Because he was trying to catch up on his sleep!

**Sometimes I tuck my knees into my chest and lean forward.**

That's just how I roll.

**Conjunctivitis.com**

Now that's a site for sore eyes.

**How many South Americans does it take to change a lightbulb?**

A Brazilian.

## A police officer caught two kids playing with a firework and a car battery.

He charged one and let the other one off.

## What is the difference between ignorance and apathy?

I don't know and I don't care.

## Dogs can't operate MRI scanners.

But catscan.

**I cut my finger chopping cheese.**

But I think that I may have grater problems.

**What do you get hanging from apple trees?**

Sore arms.

**Last night my girlfriend and I watched three DVDs back to back.**

Luckily, I was the one facing the TV.

**Never take advice from electrons.**

They are always negative.

**Why are oranges the smartest fruit?**

Because they are made to concentrate.

**What did the late tomato say to the early tomato?**

I'll ketch up

## What did the late tomato say to the early tomato?

I'll ketch up

## I have kleptomania.

But when it gets bad, I take something for it.

## I used to be addicted to soap.

But I'm clean now.

## When is a door not a door?

When it's ajar.

## I made a belt out of watches once.

It was a waist of time.

## Why did Mozart kill all his chickens?

Because when he asked them who the best composer was, they'd all say "Bach bach bach!"

**This furniture store keeps emailing me.**

All I wanted was one night stand!

**How do you find Will Smith in the snow?**

Look for fresh prints.

**I just read a book about Stockholm syndrome.**

It was pretty bad at first, but by the end I liked it.

## If at first, you don't succeed...

sky diving is not for you!

## What's large, grey, and doesn't matter?

An irrelephant.

## A book just fell on my head.

I only have my shelf to blame.

## Why can't your nose be 12 inches long?

Because then it'd be a foot.

## Have you ever heard of a music group called Cellophane?

They mostly wrap.

## What did the mountain climber name his son?

Cliff.

## Why should you never trust a pig with a secret?

Because it's bound to squeal.

## Why are mummy's scared of vacation?

They're afraid to unwind.

## What kind of dinosaur loves to sleep?

A stega-snore-us.

## When life gives you melons...

you might be dyslexic.

## What kind of tree fits in your hand?

A palm tree!

## How many tickles does it take to tickle an octopus?

Ten-tickles!

## What do you call a cow on a trampoline?

A milk shake.

DAD JOKE #230

## My boss told me to attach two pieces of wood together.

I totally nailed it!

DAD JOKE #231

## What was the pumpkin's favorite sport?

Squash.

## Recent survey revealed 6 out of 7 dwarfs aren't happy.

## What do you call corn that joins the army?

Kernel.

## I've been trying to come up with a dad joke about momentum.

But I just can't seem to get it going.

**My wife asked me to put the dog out.**

I didn't realize it was on fire.

**Every night at 11:11...**

I make a wish that someone will come fix my broken clock.

**Did you hear that the police have a warrant out on a midget psychic ripping people off?**

It reads, "Small medium at large."

**Why don't sharks eat clowns?**

Because they taste funny.

**Just read a few facts about frogs.**

They were ribbiting.

**Two satellites decided to get married.**

The wedding wasn't much, but the reception was incredible.

## What do you get if you put a duck in a cement mixer?

Quacks in the pavement.

## If you drop 1000ml of rubbish on the pavement...

you're litreing.

## They tried to make a diamond shaped like a duck.

It quacked under the pressure.

**Why do bears have hairy coats?**

Fur protection.

**What did one snowman say to the other snow man?**

Do you smell carrot?

**A vegan said to me that a person who sells meat is disgusting.**

I said people who sell fruits and vegetables are grocer.

## Why did the tree go to the dentist?

It needed a root canal.

## Why do bananas have to put on sunscreen before they go to the beach?

Because they might peel.

## What do you call a bee that lives in America?

A USB.

**I was wondering why the frisbee was getting bigger.**

Then it hit me.

**I couldn't figure out how the seat belt worked.**

Then it just clicked.

**What do you call a dad that has fallen through the ice?**

A Popsicle.

## Two parrots are sitting on a perch.

One turns to the other and asks, "do you smell fish?"

## Can a kangaroo jump higher than the Empire State Building?

Of course. The Empire State Building can't jump.

## What do you give a sick lemon?

Lemonaid.

## What do you call an old snowman?

Water.

## Why are graveyards so noisy?

Because of all the coffin.

## What kind of bagel can fly?

A plain bagel.

**What do you call a cow with no legs?**

Ground beef.

**It's hard to explain puns to kleptomaniacs.**

Because they take everything literally.

**It's difficult to say what my wife does...**

she sells sea shells by the sea shore.

DAD JOKE #262

## What did one plate say to the other plate?

Dinner is on me!

DAD JOKE #263

## What do you call a dog that can do magic tricks?

A labracadabrador.

DAD JOKE #264

## Doctor: Do you want to hear the good news or the bad news?
## Patient: Good news please.

Doctor: We're naming a disease after you.

## Atheism is a non-prophet organization.

## I called my wife and asked her if I should pick up fish and chips on the way home from work and she hung up.

She's still angry she let me name the kids.

## I tried to write a chemistry joke.

But could never get a reaction.

## What do you call a monkey in a mine field?

A babooooom!

## Want to hear a joke about construction?

Nah, I'm still working on it.

## Just watched a documentary about beavers.

It was the best damn program I've ever seen.

## You will never guess what Elsa did to the balloon.

She let it go.

## Did you hear about the two thieves who stole a calendar?

They each got six months.

## They're making a movie about clocks.

It's about time

**I've just been reading a book about anti-gravity.**

It's impossible to put down!

**Archaeology really is a career in ruins.**

**I was going to get a brain transplant.**

But I changed my mind.

**If anyone wants to come and talk about why my stuff keeps getting stolen...**

the door is always open.

**Why couldn't the lifeguard save the hippie?**

He was too far out, man.

**A woman is on trial for beating her husband to death with his guitar collection.**

**Judge says, "First offender?"**

She says, "No, first a Gibson! Then a Fender!"

**I saw an ad in a shop window, "Television for sale, $1, volume stuck on full".**

I thought, "I can't turn that down".

**I was so proud when I finished the puzzle in six months.**

On the side of the box it said three to four years.

**Where did you learn to make ice cream?**

Sundae school.

## A quick shoutout to all of the sidewalks out there.

Thanks for keeping me off the streets.

## Leather is great for sneaking around.

Because it's made of hide.

## People are making apocalypse jokes like there's no tomorrow.

## What is the tallest building in the world?

The library – it's got the most stories!

## What kind of magic do cows believe in?

MOODOO.

## What's the longest word in the dictionary?

**Smiles.**

Because there's a mile between the two S's.

**What do you call a cow with two legs?**

Lean beef.

**I never wanted to believe that my Dad was stealing from his job as a road worker.**

But when I got home, all the signs were there.

**What do you get when you cross a rabbit with a water hose?**

Hare spray.

**I applied to be a doorman but didn't get the job due to lack of experience.**

That surprised me, I thought it was an entry level position.

**I knew a guy who collected candy canes.**

They were all in mint condition.

**Why did the teddy bear say "no" to dessert?**

Because she was stuffed.

## Breaking news! Energizer Bunny arrested!

Charged with battery.

## How many bones are in the human hand?

A handful of them.

## A red and a blue ship have just collided in the Caribbean.

Apparently the survivors are marooned.

**I've just written a song about a tortilla.**

Well, it is more of a rap really.

**So, a duck walks into a pharmacy and says,**

"Give me some chap-stick... and put it on my bill"

**Toasters were the first form of pop-up notifications.**

## Which side of the chicken has more feathers?

The outside.

## Why are fish easy to weigh?

Because they have their own scales.

## Did you hear about the scientist who was lab partners with a pot of boiling water?

He had a very esteemed colleague.

**This morning I was wondering where the sun was.**

But then it dawned on me.

**I told my doctor "I've broken my arm in several places"**

He said, "Well don't go to those places."

**Two peanuts were walking down the street.**

One was a salted.

**Today a man knocked on my door and asked for a small donation towards the local swimming pool.**

I gave him a glass of water.

**What did the digital clock say to the grandfather clock?**

Look, no hands!

**Why did the melons plan a big wedding?**

Because they cantaloupe.

**Did you hear the one about the guy with the broken hearing aid?**

Neither did he.

**How was the snow globe feeling after the storm?**

A little shaken.

**What is the least spoken language in the world?**

Sign language.

**I used to think I was indecisive.**

But now I'm not sure.

**I fear for the calendar.**

Its days are numbered.

**I'm glad I know sign language.**

It's pretty handy.

**I got a female dog and named her...**

Karma.

**Our wedding was so beautiful.**

Even the cake was in tiers.

**What's the advantage of living in Switzerland?**

Well, the flag is a big plus.

## Why did the cookie cry?

It was feeling crumby.

## Where do you learn to make banana splits?

At sundae school.

## Nurse: Doctor, there's a patient that says he's invisible.

Doctor: Well, tell him I can't see him right now!

**Did you know crocodiles could grow up to 15 feet?**

But most just have 4.

**In the news a courtroom artist was arrested today.**

I'm not surprised, he always seemed sketchy.

**I used to be a banker**

But I lost interest.

**Why can't a bicycle stand on its own?**

It's two-tired.

**Astronomers got tired watching the moon go around the earth for 24 hours.**

They decided to call it a day.

**I ate a clock yesterday.**

It was so time consuming.

**Two dyslexics walk into a bra.**

**Why do scuba divers fall backwards into the water?**

Because if they fell forwards, they'd still be in the boat.

**Why did the A go to the bathroom and come out as an E?**

Because he had a vowel movement.

**Never trust someone with graph paper.**

They're always plotting something.

**What do you call a group of disorganized cats?**

A cat-tastrophe.

**Why can't you hear a pterodactyl go to the bathroom?**

The p is silent.

## What's the worst part about being a cross-eyed teacher?

They can't control their pupils.

## Someone broke into my house last night and stole my limbo trophy.

How low can you go?

## Mountains aren't just funny.

They're hill areas.

**I was going to learn how to juggle.**

But I didn't have the balls.

**Every machine in the coin factory broke down all of a sudden without explanation.**

It just doesn't make any cents.

**If you want a job in the moisturizer industry.**

The best advice I can give is to apply daily.

**When you have a bladder infection.**

Urine trouble.

**What happens when you offend a brain surgeon?**

They will give you a piece of your mind.

**The first time I got a universal remote control I thought to myself...**

This changes everything!

## Why did the man put his money in the freezer?

He wanted cold hard cash!

## I decided to sell my vacuum.

It was just collecting dust.

## Why do ducks make great detectives?

They always quack the case.

**I bought shoes from a drug dealer once.**

I don't know what he laced them with, but I was tripping all day.

**What do vegetarian zombies eat?**

Grrrrrainnnnnssss.

**What is the hardest part about sky diving?**

The ground.

**There's not really any training for garbagemen.**

They just pick things up as they go.

**Did you hear about the cow who jumped over the barbed wire fence?**

It was udder destruction.

**What do you call a bear with no teeth?**

A gummy bear!

**I've deleted the phone numbers of all the Germans I know from my mobile phone.**

Now it's Hans free.

**What's the best thing about elevator jokes?**

They work on so many levels.

**Two fish are in a tank, one turns to the other and says...**

"How do you drive this thing?"

**I finally bought the limited-edition Thesaurus that I've always wanted.**

**When I opened it, all the pages were blank.**

I have no words to describe how angry I am.

**This is my step ladder.**

I never knew my real ladder.

**I was thinking about moving to Moscow.**

But there is no point Russian into things.

**I got an A on my origami assignment when I turned my paper into my teacher.**

**My wife got angry at me for kicking the dropped ice cubes under the refrigerator.**

But now it's all just water under the fridge.

## Why did the scarecrow win an award?

Because he was outstanding in his field.

## Americans can't switch from pounds to kilograms overnight.

That would cause mass confusion.

## A man got hit in the head with a can of Coke.

But he was alright because it was a soft drink.

**A man walked into a bar with some asphalt on his arm.**

He said, "Two beers please, one for me and one for the road."

**I'll tell you something about German sausages...**

They're the wurst.

**What do prisoners use to call each other?**

Cell phones.

## What's E.T. short for?

He's only got little legs.

## Today a girl said she recognized me from vegetarian club.

But I'm sure I've never met herbivore.

## How do you make holy water?

You boil the hell out of it.

## Did you hear about the submarine industry?

It really took a dive...

## Why do pirates not know the alphabet?

They always get stuck at "C".

## Why did the house go to the doctor?

It was having window panes.

## I've invented a new word

Plagiarism

## I wouldn't buy anything with Velcro.

It's a total rip-off.

## Why do crabs never give to charity?

Because they're shellfish.

**How do you make a hankie dance?**

Put a little boogie in it.

**The other day I was listening to a song about superglue.**

It's been stuck in my head ever since.

**The great thing about stationery shops...**

is that they're always in the same place.

## What's red and bad for your teeth?

A brick.

## I heard there was a new store called Moderation.

They have everything there.

## I used to work for a soft drink can crusher.

It was soda pressing.

## Why did the chicken get a penalty?

For fowl play.

## My cat was just sick on the carpet.

I don't think it's feline well.

## Why did the burglar hang his mugshot on the wall?

To prove that he was framed!

**I dreamed about drowning in an ocean made out of orange soda last night.**

It took me a while to work out it was just a Fanta sea.

**I heard there was a new store called Moderation.**

They have everything there.

**I used to work for a soft drink can crusher.**

It was soda pressing.

## What do you call a nervous javelin thrower?

Shakespeare.

## I had a dream that I was a muffler last night.

I woke up exhausted!

## I broke my finger at work today.

On the other hand I'm completely fine.

## Why did the worker get fired from the orange juice factory?

Lack of concentration.

## I couldn't get a reservation at the library.

They were completely booked.

## What do you call an Argentinian with a rubber toe?

Roberto

**I went to the zoo the other day, there was only one dog in it.**

It was a shitzu.

**I gave all my dead batteries away today...**

Free of charge.

**Why didn't the number 4 get into the nightclub?**

Because he is 2 square.

## Past, present, and future walked into a bar...

It was tense.

## Did you hear about the bread factory burning down?

They say the business is toast.

## Why are skeletons so calm?

Because nothing gets under their skin.

## Have you heard about the film "Constipation"?

You probably haven't because it's not out yet.

## My friend said to me: "What rhymes with orange"

I said: "no it doesn't"

## What did the one eye say to the other eye?

Hey, between you and me... something smells!

DAD JOKE #402

**I woke up in the middle of the night to see the ghost of Gloria Gaynor in my bedroom.**

At first, I was afraid. I was petrified.

DAD JOKE #403

**All cucumbers are sea cucumbers.**

Otherwise they'd be ucumbers

DAD JOKE #404

**Want to hear my pizza joke?**

Never mind, it's too cheesy.

## Cosmetic surgery used to be such a taboo subject.

Now you can talk about Botox and nobody raises an eyebrow.

## I asked a Frenchman if he played video games.

He said, "Wii"

## Shout out to my grandma!

That's the only way she can hear me.

## What do you call an alligator in a vest?

An in-vest-igator.

## Thanks for explaining the word "many" to me.

It means a lot.

## What biscuit does a short person like?

Shortbread.

**What's 50 Cent's name in Zimbabwe?**

200 Dollars.

**Gravity's one of the most fundamental forces in the universe. What do you get when you remove it?**

Gravy.

**My sea sickness comes in waves.**

**For Valentine's day, I decided to get my wife some beads for an abacus.**

It's the little things that count.

**What's the worst thing about ancient history class?**

The teachers tend to Babylon.

**My new thesaurus is terrible.**

In fact, it's so bad, I'd say it's terrible.

**Dad died because he couldn't remember his blood type. I will never forget his last words.**

Be positive.

**Why didn't the orange win the race?**

It ran out of juice.

**Why did the Clydesdale give the pony a glass of water?**

Because he was a little horse!

## Why shouldn't you smoke medicinal marijuana during a thunderstorm?

Because lightning strikes the highest object.

What did the Buffalo say to his little boy when he dropped him off at school?

Bison.

## I used to have a job at a calendar factory.

But I got the sack because I took a couple of days off.

**I wish I could clean mirrors for a living.**

It's just something I can see myself doing.

**How do the trees get on the internet?**

They log on.

**To the guy who invented zero...**

Thanks for nothing.

## What lies at the bottom of the ocean and twitches?

A nervous wreck.

## We all know Albert Einstein was a genius.

But his brother Frank was a monster.

## My girlfriend dated a clown right before she met me.

I've got some big shoes to fill.

## Does refusing to go to the gym count as resistance training?

## What do you call a bulletproof Irishman?

Rick O'Shea

## Stephen King has a son named Joe.

I'm not joking, but he is.

## What's Iron Man without his suit?

Stark Naked

DAD JOKE #433

## I tripped over my wife's bra.

It was a booby trap.

DAD JOKE #434

## What do you call a sad cup of coffee?

Depresso.

**Never marry a tennis player.**

Love means nothing to them.

**I accidentally swallowed some string last night.**

I shit you knot.

**Did you know Darth Vader has a sister?**

Her name is Ella.

## I told my doctor I was constipated.

He said, "Yea, no shit".

## What does a house wear?

Address.

## I was once attacked by a group of mimes.

They did unspeakable things to me.

**I lose 20% of my couch.**

ouch.

**My wife didn't believe me when I said that I would give our daughter a silly name.**

So I decided to call her Bluff.

**I asked 100 women which shampoo they preferred.**

All of them replied: "How the hell did you get in here?"

**I threw a party for all the workers who helped build my house. The door guy showed up late.**

But he really knew how to make an entrance.

**I would avoid the sushi if I was you.**

It's a little fishy.

**A scarecrow says, "This job isn't for everyone.**

But hay, it's in my jeans."

**3 guys are on a boat with 4 cigarettes but nothing to light them with. So, they throw one cigarette overboard and the boat**

becomes a cigarette lighter.

**I used to be afraid of hurdles**

But I got over it.

**Don't trust people that do acupuncture.**

They're back stabbers.

**Why was Dumbo sad?**

He felt irrelephant.

**Why can't two elephants go swimming?**

Because they only have one pair of trunks.

**The inventor of the throat lozenge has died.**

There will be no coffin at his funeral

**Daughter: "Daddy, why didn't I get a sunburn?"**

**Dad: "You can't, honey?"**

**Daughter: "Really?"**

Dad: "You can only get a daughterburn."

**My wife said me she hated her hair cut.**

I told her: "Don't worry, it'll grow on you."

## I'll do algebra, tackle geometry, maybe even a little calculus...

But graphing is where I draw the line.

## What kind of shoes do ninjas wear?

Sneakers

## A guy walked into a bar...

And was disqualified from the limbo contest.

**I used to have a job collecting leaves.**

I was raking it in.

**The doctor told me, "Sorry for the wait!"**

I replied, "It's alright, I'm patient."

**What happens if a frog parks illegally?**

They get toad.

## Did you know that cannibals won't eat clowns?

They taste funny.

## If Watson isn't the most famous doctor in the world.

Then who is.

## My dog Minton has eaten all of my shuttlecocks.

Badminton.

## Why is it good luck to say 'break a leg' to an actor?

Because every play needs a cast.

## You know why aliens haven't visited us yet?

They checked our reviews. One star.

## I was on the toilet last night when the clock struck midnight.

I thought to myself, "same shit, different day".

**Would anyone be interested in being my companion?**

Asking for a friend.

**Spent $400 on a limo, but I didn't get a driver for it.**

All that money, and nothing to chauffeur it.

**My wife is mad that I keep introducing her as "my ex-girlfriend".**

## I taught my daughter what a bargain meant.

She said, "Thanks dad, that means a great deal".

## Did you know the first French Fries weren't cooked in France?

They were actually cooked in Greece.

## I applied to be a pilot.

But I couldn't land the job.

**My wife asked me to choose between our relationship and my career as a reporter.**

Boy, do I have some news for her.

**It's probably not safe for me to be driving my car right now.**

But hey, bad brakes have never stopped me before.

**Why did the DJ go to the farmers' market?**

To get some fresh beets.

**Space heaters are the best house-warming gifts.**

**I think my wife is secretly putting glue on my antique weapon collection.**

She denies it, but I'm sticking to my guns.

**What did the mermaid wear to her math class?**

An algae bra.

**I don't understand why some people use fractions instead of decimals.**

It's pointless.

**Why do dentists call them "dental x-rays" when they could just call them...**

Tooth pics.

**My wife says I'm addicted to drinking brake fluid.**

Joke's on her. I can stop whenever I want.

**I had a dream about mufflers.**

I woke up exhausted.

**Don't you hate it when someone answers their own questions?**

I do.

**How do you know a witch's car is coming?**

You can hear 'broom broom'.

**I love jokes about the eyes.**

The cornea the better.

**My friend keeps saying, "cheer up man, it could be worse. You could be stuck underground in a hole full of water".**

I know he means well.

**I never understood why people dislike vegans so much.**

I have never had beef with them.

## What is a web developer's favorite tea?

URL Grey

## Son: I have an imaginary girlfriend.

## Dad: You know... you could do a lot better, right?

## Son: Thanks dad, that means a lot.

Dad: I wasn't talking to you. I was talking to your girlfriend.

**Got my dream job today. I get my own 200-thousand-dollar company car and a corner window with a view of the city.**

Being a city bus driver is a dream come true.

**I can't believe I was arrested for impersonating a politician.**

I was just sitting there doing nothing.

**My wife and I have three beautiful children.**

Three out of five isn't bad...

DAD JOKE #493

**Never challenge Death to a pillow fight.**

Unless you're prepared to handle the reaper cushions.

DAD JOKE #494

**Today was my first day as a pilot. I looked down nervously and asked, "What are all these buttons for?"**

My co-pilot sighed, "Those are to keep your shirt closed".

DAD JOKE #495

**It takes guts to be an organ donor.**

**I'm developing a phobia of German sausage.**

I fear the wurst

**Someone stole my mood ring.**

I don't know how I feel about that.

**Every morning I announce loudly to my family that I'm going jogging, but then don't go.**

It's a running joke.

I just saw my math teacher lock himself in his office with a piece of graph paper.

**I think he must be plotting something.**

# DAD JOKE #500

**When does a joke become a dad joke?**

When it becomes apparent.

Printed in Poland
by Amazon Fulfillment
Poland Sp. z o.o., Wrocław